This Belongs to:

All rights reserved.

2021 Edition

"If you have one foot in yesterday and one foot in tomorrow, you're pissing all over today."
- Michael J. Fox

BACK TO THE FUTURE

MICHAEL J. FOX
THE SECRET OF MY
SUCCESS

Bright Lights,
Big City.

Teen Wolf

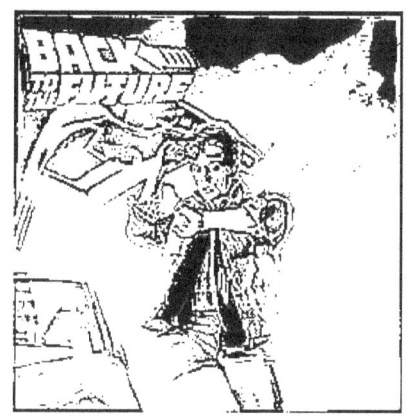

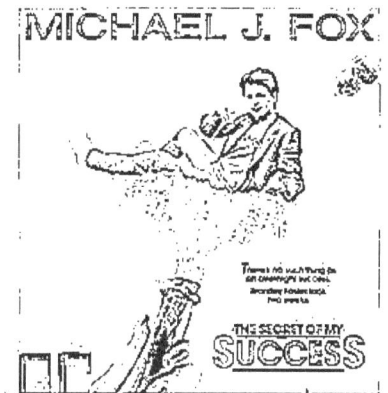

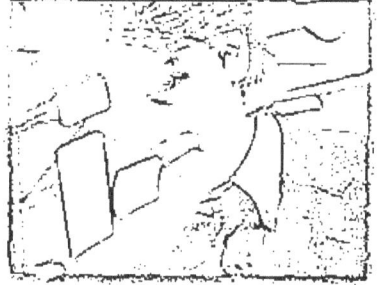

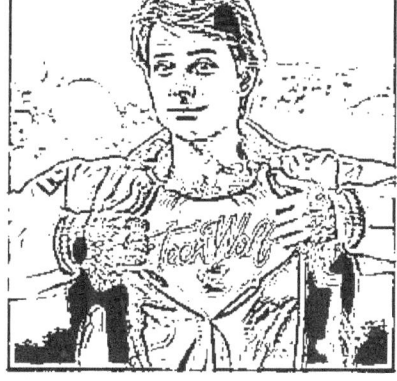

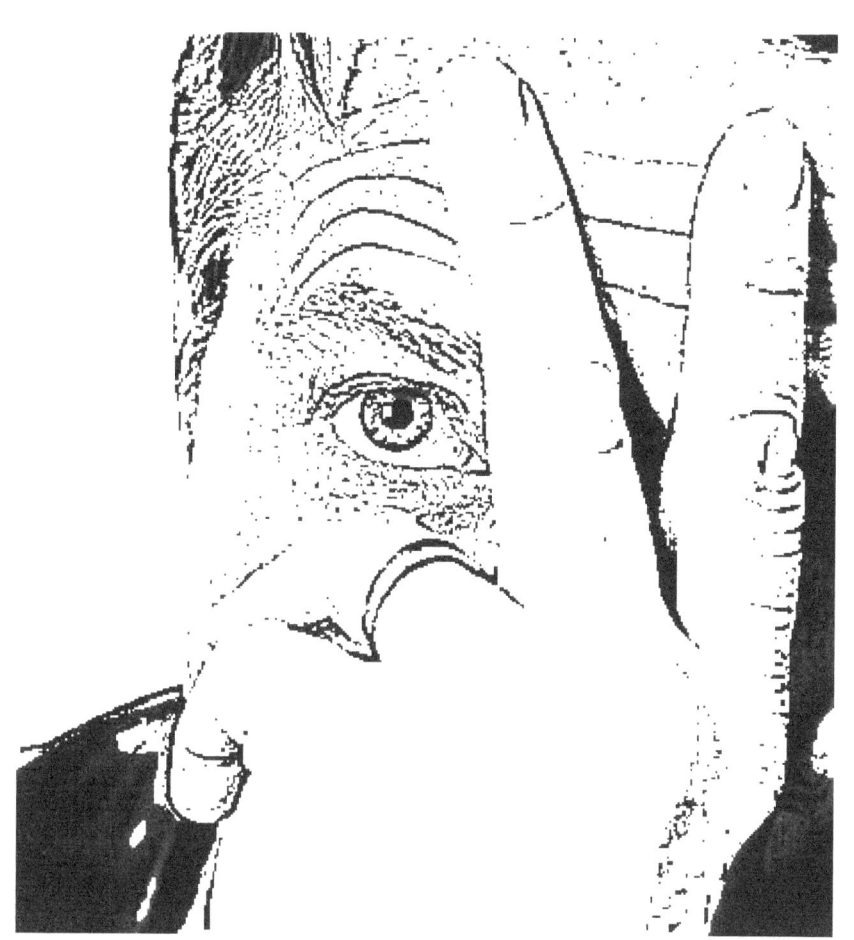

GQ

For the Modern Man/December $3.00

The Rise
And Rise
Of
Michael
J. Fox

THE NEW LUXURY

A Guide to Living Sinfully

Formal Wear With Flair

The Drinking Man's Diet

The (Mmmmm) Massage: Beyond Pleasure

The Death Of Hip

CPSIA information can be obtained
at www.ICGtesting.com
Printed in the USA
LVHW050157171220
674342LV00009B/2186